Lady Muck

Lady Muck

BY
William Mayne
Illustrated
by
Jonathan Heale

E
MAY

HOUGHTON MIFFLIN COMPANY
BOSTON   1997

For Little Pig Robinson
—W.M.

For Mary
—J.H.

Text copyright © 1997 by William Mayne
Illustrations copyright © 1997 by Jonathan Heale

First American edition published by Houghton Mifflin Company.
First published in Great Britain by Reed Children's Books Ltd.

For information about this and other Houghton Mifflin
trade and reference books and multimedia products, visit
The Bookstore at Houghton Mifflin on the World Wide Web
at http://www.hmco.com/trade/.

Printed in Hong Kong
Produced by Mandarin Offset Ltd

10 9 8 7 6 5 4 3 2 1

Library of Congress Cataloging-in-Publication Data
Mayne, William
Lady Muck / by William Mayne;
illustrated by Joanthan Heale. — 1st American ed.
p. cm.
Summary: Sowk and Boark, two greedy pigs, plot to become rich
from the sale of the truffles they have found in the woods,
but their greed proves to be their undoing.
ISBN 0-395-75281-7
[1. Pigs—Fiction. 2. Greed—Fiction.] I. Title.
PZ7.M4736Lad 1997 [E]—dc20 95-14009 CIP AC

Lady Muck

A pig named Boark lived in the mud, and one day to his wife he said, "Sowk, my Sowk, what can I do to please and happy you, my Sowky dear?"

"Oink," said she, "go snuffly and diggy fat sweet rooties. That will happy me, Boark, my Boarky dear, from grunt to squeal." Walkies were such trouble to her fat old sides and breath, and strained her little eyes so.

She sat in her damp and sticky black wallow, and off he plodded to sniffle out tender twirls of skirret and carrot and parsnip and even a potatio.

Under the beech trees he snuffled, and he came upon, oh, the whifflom of the greatest pigly tasties, down under the woodland mold.

"Don't hidy there," he said. "I know you be lurking, little snack and dinner, little snap and supper." And he set to, more sniffly yet, to find the nest of those best things.

Back at the farm, up got Sowk from the muddy place, scratched belly with foot, rubbed her backside upon a tree to wake it up, and twirl-and-twitched her piggy tail till it went twang and sat up smart.

"That be Sowky ready for off," said she, and trotted off nim-nim to the field; but no Boark in the field. She wanted what he snuffled, so when she got her breath she went trit-trot down the lane to the yard; yet no Boark in the yard.

"Boarky," she called, but he couldn't hear, away down in the beechwood, listening to the tasties underground, sniffling with his flat nose.

Sowk went to the woods, bumpety bump, grunt and puff, like a rock snoring, tail ringing like a bell.

"Boarky," she called again, all gasping with shake-up-and-down, and breathless as lard — but no reply.

Boark didn't hear, slothering his chops at a row of magic smell he sniffled down below.

"Get 'em ate before dear Sowk land down," he said, his little old tail losing all its curl with greed.

He put down his snout and delved in the beech-leaves for that smell strong as love, wonderful, wonderful, waiting down in the roots.

"Get at it I will," said Boark. "Never see this much smell but once in a lifey and all mine, all miney."

He took a look round, the old sly, and he didn't see dearest Sowk, and digged and dribbled on.

"There he do seek," said Sowk, running down on him like, oh, like a mudslide, shouting, "Boarky, Boarky, what did you find for your Sowky? With your scrapy and your snuffly and your dig, tusk, dig?"

"Not found naught yet," said Boarky, "my love," said he, his snout, oh, an inch from Paradise. "Naught here, not a scrappy, just my fancy." Well, he thought, plenty for one, and me find it, I did. "Nothing, Sowk, my Sowky, naught."

But Sowk had the scent now. "Dig, diggy," she said. "On with snuffle, and dig out a truffle."

Truffles were what Boark found, truffles best to eat of all he could find. Boark would eat them now, but Sowk knew that truffles were better in the market where folk pay for them in goldy round money.

"Get a truffly out," she said. "Gently as babby piggy, lay it to one side. We won't eat that. There'll be better."

"There be naught better," said Boark. "Don't it please my Sowk, my Sowky dear, to eat a truffly from her hubby? Just one truffly?"

"It please her dreadful," said Sowk. "It please her from silk ear to scratch back. Find another and anothery, Boark, my Boarky deary. Findy more again."

Boark got the little thing out, and set it down, no bigger than apple down from tree, but smell, oh, like orchard of heaven.

"Eaty that, Sowk my love, my Sowky," he said, sad to his pig heart to say it to Sowky, his other love. "I get a littly one for me, all I ever need."

"Eaty naught and none," said Sowk, turning that thing with her lovely snout. "We go to market and sell trufflies for gold."

"Ah," said Boark. "And we buy bigger trufflies of our own."

"No, no," said Sowk. "Diggy on, diggy down, Boarky. We rich folk now, lady and gentlepiggies. We buy coach to ride about the country, grand as duchy and duchessy."

"We been born for better thingies," said Boark. "Yes, my Sowky, so we was." Down went his snout, and flap went his ears, but his heart twitched, oh, just a little miserable. "You said it many times and many."

"I always feeled it in my chop and chine," said Sowk. "One day the worldy know what we are."

"And here come next truffly," said Boark, and brought out another like the first, like a norange, like a potatio.

"One each," said Sowk. "Oh my souly and oh my belly. Here it come hard. Be strong, Sowk."

"Be strong, Sowky dear," said Boark. "I've finded the nesty and the babbies in it, onc, two, three, from old to youngy."

"Oh my gammon and my flitch," said Sowk. "Oh my bacon and my rind."

Boark's tongue longed to lick, his jaws to bite, chew and chewy, and throat to swallow-swallowy! But he laid that tender family in a basket, two bigs, a middle, a little middly, and the babbies.

"We'll buy a coachman too," said Sowk, counting all. "Ready and running. And be such a show on silky cushies."

Off they went to market. Folks turned their heads at the strong and eaty smell like banquet, going down the road.

Sowk felt a little peckish on the way, just by the old churchy, oh, that steeple took some walking by on a hot day like this, tiry ways and long road.

That babbiest of truffles is such a fussy, oh, so rolling about in the basket, thought Sowk. Best nursey him a bit. I been a mother, I know.

Out he came, all breathless. "Looky the view," said Sowk. "Hear the bells a-ringing in the city."

"Very and right pretty," said Boark.

But Sowk didn't speak to him. She spoke to the truffle babby.

"Let's just snuffly you," she whisper-whispery to him, and has him up by her snouty and a-kissing him before he can say helpy. "No need to be frighty," said Sowk.

But he was frighted, jumping in among her teeth, running down the red lane to tummy, and happy there.

Rest of the family forgot to notice, and never big talkers, born to be silent under the beech-tree roots. Boark saw nothing and had naught to say.

"Tidied up the old basket," said Sowk to herself. "Look bettery now."

In a while, at the bridge across the wide river, "That wetty below sets me in mind of thirsty and that," said Sowk. She looked to see the other babbies sitting comfy, and just one maybe took the journey hard.

"You ridy insidy." said Sowk, "with your brothery or sistery."

"We get no coachy yet," said Boark.

"Not you, Boark, my Boarky dear," said Sowk, when that tiresome babby got off her tongue and sat quiet down below.

"Getting along well," said Boark. "Be in the market today, we tritty and we trotty."

"Not too cold and not too hotty," said Sowk, licking a lippy.

Then came the crossroads, and "My how hoppity they trufflies be," said Sowk. "Stop playing gamies, you'll get bruises and they won't a-like you none down in the market."

"Carry careful," said Boark.

Sowk took a look for bruises. "Just in casey," said she to herself, "tasty this truffly just as hasty and no wasty." And down it went.

They came to the town ditch and had to wait at the gate. "Those trufflies getting tired," said Sowk.

"Keep them in the shady," said Boark.

Sowk popped one inside in the shady. "Me myself I worry for," she said. "But I keepy going, I do."

At town not so many notice.

"They don't smell so strong adown here," said Boark.
"Proud folks, or littly smell or trufflies all asleepy-oh."

"It's the airy," said Sowk. "That never so good in townie.
That it'll be." But she knew it wasn't that. No, not at all.

They got in the market, and put up a stall.

"Boark will go and find us dinnery," said Boark.

"Well, kindly, Boark, my Boark dear," said Sowk. "Don't
trouble with none for I, because the walk do weary Sowk, and
she will wait and waity until she ridy home on coachy."

Off Boarky went to rootle and to firkle and to find. Sowk sat by the stall and waited. And Boark did not come back, and he did not come.

"What a time my Boarky dear do take," said Sowk.

Still he didn't come, still he stayed away, and Sowk looked to see how they were wearing down in the basket, just the pair of them by now.

"The littlie ones inside weepy for their mammy, like any babby," said Sowk. "Which one be mammy?" She looked, thought, and made up her mind.

"Must be righty," she said, when all was quietly down there, no weepy, no snuffly, no jumpy.

Boarky came back. "Naught and none to eaty in town streety," he said, a bit patchy-tempered. Then he smiled, because he saw but one and only truffle in the basket. "You selled four or fivey," he said. "You got goldy for them?"

"They didn't travelly too goody," said Sowk. "Boark, oh my Boarky dear. They been deadly quarrelsome." And she dropped a porky little tear.

But he wasn't cross. "And that naughty one ate up the rest, then?" said he, and so he thought.

Well, that was easy, thought Sowk, and he would be so cross if he knowed. "Something of the sorty," she said. "We'll get him soldy and buy the coachy but not a coachy man. If you ride up in your wiggy with your whippy I shall wave trotter like queeny."

27

But when the truffle went to a cook-man for his café, there came only a little brown money, hardly a silvery, and not any goldy round sort.

All that Boark can buy, all that Sowk can ride in, is a wheelybarrow, old farmery wheelybarrow.

"How you get so heavy in a day when you eaty naught and none beat me," said Boark, pushing Sowk out of town, across the bridge, over the crossroads, and past the churchy tower.

The people at home called out, "Well ridden, Lady Muck, Lady Mucky."

"See," said Sowk, "Lady Muck get respect and ordinary Mrs. Muck never come near that. We come up in the world even with a wheelybarrow."

Then the wheely broke and the barrow split, and Sowk pitched out into the ditch of sticky mud.

"This happy Sowk," said Sowk, "in a muddy and a wallowy, and she never, ever, have such a day for swallowy."

"I love to make you happy, Sowk, my Sowky dear," said Boark.

"And so I am happy," said Sowk, and her tail drooped with joy. "So I am, from brawn to bristle, from chap to chitterling."

"We might as well have eaten just one eachy," said Boark, "of those dratty trufflies and their quarrelly ways."

"I wouldn't a-let you," said Sowk, forgetting in the ditch.

"Nor I wouldn't a-let you," said Boark, "though you are my Sowky, Sowk, Sowk, and all lovely with muddy, my true Lady Muck."

"Oink," said Lady Muck.